D1162213

65p

Grandpa Bear's Blossom Shop:
© 1974 Thomas Nelson & Sons Limited
ISBN 72381039 7
Printed in Great Britain by A. Wheaton & Co., Exeter.

GRANDPA BEAR'S BLOSSOM SHOP

By Gerda Macaskie

Illustrated by Ben and Stephanie Manchipp

NELSON
YOUNG WORLD

Tiny Bear cycled up to Grandpa Bear's
Blossom Shop. He was very excited. It was
Saturday and he didn't have to go to school,
so he was going to help his Grandpa.

"I'm so pleased you've come," said Grandpa. "I am very busy today so you can help with deliveries. This bouquet of roses is for Mrs. Honeybear. It is her birthday today."

Besides the roses, there were a lot of other flowers
to deliver. Some of them were birthday gifts, some
thank-you gifts and some surprise gifts. So Tiny
carefully loaded them all on to the carrier of his bike.

He felt very important as he rode along with all those flowers, and as he passed his friends they would wave at him and say, "Look at Tiny, doesn't he look busy, he must be helping his Grandpa deliver all those flowers."

He decided to deliver the roses first, so he left his bike outside Mrs. Honeybear's pretty cottage and knocked on the door.

When Mrs. Honeybear opened the door, Tiny Bear wished her many happy returns of the day and handed her the roses. "What a wonderful surprise!" she cried.

As he made his way down Mrs. Honeybear's garden he noticed a flower that he had never seen before. Tiny decided he would ask Grandpa what it could be.

Tiny delivered the rest of the flowers and went back to the shop. He was longing to ask Grandpa about the flowers, but Grandpa was very busy. There was going to be a big wedding in the village church that afternoon, and Grandpa was making all the bouquets, posies and buttonholes.

Tiny liked the bride's
bouquet. There were some
carnations, like the one
Grandpa had in his button-
hole, and some lovely
fresh green ferns. Grandpa
Bear had made it look very
pretty.

Grandpa Bear asked Tiny if he would deliver a bowl of hyacinths to old Mrs. Growlybear. It was her birthday, too, and the hyacinths were a present from her family who lived a long way away. "Of course I will," said Tiny Bear. "Mrs. Growlybear will like them very much."

Tiny Bear was right. Mrs. Growlybear was delighted with the hyacinths. "Come in, Tiny," she said. "I expect you'd like a cup of tea after all your hard work!"

Mrs. Growlybear took Tiny into her nice, homely kitchen. Then she made a big pot of tea and got out some nice crusty bread. It was thickly spread with butter and honey, and to follow there were some of Mrs. Growlybear's delicious home-made cakes. All that cycling had given Tiny Bear quite an appetite.

When Tiny Bear got back to the shop, there
on the table was a big bunch of the flowers
he had seen in Mrs. Honeybear's garden. "Grandpa,"
he cried, "what are these flowers called? I must
know all the flowers' names." "Ha," said Grandpa,
"they are called lilac and are going to be used to
decorate the church hall for the wedding reception.

Would you deliver them for me?" "Oh, yes," said Tiny.
There was also a big bunch of roses to be delivered
to Mrs. Bruinbear. Tiny loved roses. They looked as if they
were made of velvet.

What a busy day Tiny Bear was having. He put
the lilac and roses on his bike and set off once
again. But the poor little bear was getting very
tired. He couldn't remember who the lilac was
for and where he had to take the roses to. "I think
Grandpa said that the lilac was for Mrs. Bruinbear
and the roses for the church," he said.

When he got to the church Tiny Bear was still not sure. "I think it must be the roses," he said at last. "I'll leave them here in the doorway. That's what Grandpa told me to do."

Then Tiny Bear made his way to Mrs. Bruinbear's house with the lilac that he thought she had ordered. He noticed some lovely hyacinths growing in her garden and he stooped down to smell them.

When Mrs. Bruinbear saw that Tiny Bear had brought some lilac for her she threw up her hands in horror. There is an old belief that it is unlucky to have lilac in the house. "I didn't order lilac," she told Tiny Bear. "I ordered roses!"

But Mrs. Bruinbear thought that Tiny Bear looked
so tired and sad, and the lilac did smell so lovely,
that she said: "That's all right Tiny Bear, they
do look beautiful," and without another word she
took the flowers inside.

Tiny Bear went back to the
shop and found the only flowers
left to deliver were a big
bunch of violets. They were
for his Mother. Tomorrow
was Mothering Sunday!

As Tiny Bear was cycling home, he passed the church. The wedding had just finished and everyone was outside having their photographs taken. Tiny Bear noticed all the lovely flowers—the bride's bouquet, the bridesmaids' posies, and all the buttonholes—and he remembered that they had all come from his Grandpa's shop and that he had helped to get them ready.
He did feel proud.